I0818048

The Key To The City

Lynda Corrado

Dedication

This book is dedicated to the life and sacrifices of our Founding Fathers, who fought tirelessly to establish democracy after years of oppression under autocratic rule.

Thomas Jefferson reflected on the Declaration of Independence and made it clear that the purpose was not to be entirely original. It was meant to explain the reasoning behind the American colonies and demonstrate the American way of thinking. Jefferson emphasized that the authority of the Declaration relied on the prevailing sentiments of the time. He completed his defense of "life, liberty, and the pursuit of happiness" in just two weeks, undergoing the typical editing process. The Committee of Five and the Second Continental

Congress made many changes to the document, even removing entire sections. The final version of the Declaration of Independence includes a preamble, a list of grievances, a formal declaration of independence, and signatures. The Declaration highlights the importance of individual rights, particularly the belief in the equality of all individuals and their inherent, inalienable rights: life, liberty, and the pursuit of happiness.

National Historical Society of Pennsylvania

Lynda Corrado, a determined and ambitious Capricorn, has led a nomadic life, traversing vibrant landscapes that have allowed her to connect with individuals from diverse backgrounds. The crisp mountain air surrounded her as she taught skiing and the power of the waves and wind while sailing, immersing herself in the exhilarating rush of these outdoor activities. Alongside these roles, she embraced the elegance of her work as a concierge, navigating the bustling sounds of hotel lobbies.

However, it was during her time as the founder of the first all-women's team in the America's Cup that Corrado's path took an unexpected turn. In the late

1990s, while engrossed in research on term limits, she stumbled upon a website discussing ancient Greek democracy. The glow of her computer screen illuminated her face as she dove deeper into the intricacies of this historical system. This serendipitous encounter sparked an idea within her, igniting a fire that would drive her to embark on a literary journey.

Contemplating the necessary steps to transform her vision of self-governance in urban settings into reality, Corrado found her fingers dancing across the keyboard, capturing her thoughts.

Driven by the profound importance of her quest, Corrado decides to write a novel that transcends mere words on a page. She strives to immerse people in the sights, sounds, and emotions of their own communities, awakening them to the value they hold in serving their fellow citizens. With every keystroke, she aims to reveal the true power that resides within each individual, empowering them to shape government policies and create a brighter future for all.

Table of Contents

Introduction

As a New Yorker, Dr. Maxine Caldwell knew a thing or two about navigating a jungle. Not a literal one, but the urban kind—where a fierce determination ignites within you the moment you step onto the bustling streets. She carried that same energy with her as she stood in the busy airport terminal, her heart racing with an excitement that felt both overwhelming and real.

Surrounded by the symphony of echoing announcements and the rush of travelers, her mind wandered to the retired lawyer from her neighborhood. Her encouragement had been the golden key, unlocking the gateway to this international adventure. She pictured herself beneath brilliant stage lights, the roar of a worldwide audience washing over her. The vision of that prestigious medal resting on her chest filled her with a tidal wave of pride and humility, so intense it nearly swept her off her feet. This was the moment she had dreamed of, the moment she was finally stepping into.

Chapter 1 - The Descent

The captain's voice echoed through the cabin. "Ladies and gentlemen, we are about to begin our descent into Oslo International Airport. Please fasten your seat belts."

Dr. Maxine Caldwell gazed out the window as Norway's wild beauty unfurled below. The deep, crystalline water swept her back to a sunlit regatta in Bergen, where memories shimmered as brightly as the fjords. She could still picture the lush, emerald hills, breathe in the air so pure it tingled on her tongue, and recall the committee boat adrift, unable to anchor in the fathomless depths.

Her thoughts drifted to the locals, so warm and welcoming that they made her feel like royalty. They'd even given her a nickname, “Queenie,” the very same one her father had bestowed upon her years ago. She smiled at the thought. Her father hadn't called her that because he saw a princess.

He’d seen her take charge. After her mother left, their family life had been a mess, and someone had to step up. When he came home from work each night, her father would ask her sister, “What kind of mood is Queenie in tonight?” The nickname wasn't just a label; it was a source of strength, a reminder of the assertive, creative personality she'd had to develop to get by. She’d learned to summon that queen within whenever self-doubt threatened to consume her.

This "gift" of hers—the ability to conjure a creative visual from her mind at a moment's notice—had always amazed her sister. But her teachers hadn't called it a gift. They had called it **Attention Deficit Disorder**.

The memory of a superintendent in the school system where she taught, who also had ADD, came to mind. He had left her alone, allowing her to have free rein in her classroom at an alternative school in the projects—a last stop before

Juvie for many of her students. Her lessons were unconventional. She hadn't been good with memorizing formulas, which was why she'd struggled with high school math. Yet, here she was, teaching math and science. She focused on helping students truly understand the concepts of numbers before introducing any formulas. She called them "shortcuts," and because of her approach, her students' test scores were exceptional, far surpassing expectations.

She remembered a summer weekend spent splashing Peacock Blue across her classroom walls, swapping out battered desks for round tables that invited conversation and creativity. Teaching had never been her dream; her father had nudged her toward it, dismissing her wish to be an architect as impractical. In his eyes, a woman belonged in the kitchen, not in a career that demanded costly schooling he reserved for his son. She honored her roots, but her spirit yearned for more. So she learned to ski, and with that bold step, launched herself on a quest for independence. She left New York behind, flying to San Francisco, a lone traveler in an unfamiliar world. Alone, yes, but for the first time, she felt the exhilarating freedom of self-reliance. The journey had been long and lonely, but as the plane dipped toward Oslo, she felt certain: every twist and turn had brought her to this hard-won, luminous moment.

Chapter 2 - The Creation

"Dr. Caldwell," a gentle voice broke through the hum of the airplane, pulling me from my reverie. I looked up to see a stewardess standing beside my seat, her posture graceful and confident.

"A black limousine awaits you beyond baggage claim, at gate number four. Just turn left as you disembark."

I longed to stay adrift in my daydream, gliding on the bright currents of possibility. I knew that the moment I landed, reality would pull me back to earth. So I let my mind drift to the past, to the days when I imagined myself as a syndicated columnist. In those years, I juggled ski lessons and concierge shifts, but my true passion was sparked by the news, always searching for a story that would set my pen ablaze. Again and again, one debate rose above the rest: the issue of term limits in Congress.

My research led me to ancient Greek civilization—a memory that immediately brought me back to my sister and our old black-and-white television. On Saturday mornings, we'd watch tales of Greek mythology, completely enthralled by the Gods of Mount Olympus. That fascination reemerged as I learned about ancient Greek democracy, which had term limits to ensure every male citizen had a chance to represent the people. The concept was beautiful in its simplicity.

This vision of genuine civic participation spun through my mind for over twenty years, a persistent thread I could never quite tie to reality. I had chased plenty of ideas that promised fortune, but this one tugged at me differently. When I finally returned to New York City, I felt compelled to act. Hunter College's urban development program called to me, and as I scanned their course listings, a summer studio project leapt off the page—a rare opportunity to help shape a real community.

In that instant, everything fell into place. I realized I did not need to be a tenured professor to spark change. I could shape lives as an associate professor while pursuing my doctorate. Energized by this newfound clarity, I marched straight to the Dean of Urban Renewal and scheduled a meeting.

And that's how the **Thrive America Plan** was born. I recall the humid summer air, the honking taxis, and the constant energy of the city as I entered my first class. The smell of freshly printed handouts, the chatter of excited students—it was all so alive. That summer, with twenty hand-picked students, the city became our classroom. We walked its streets, not just as New Yorkers, but as pioneers. My vision for TAP began to take shape with every step, every conversation, every detail we absorbed.

Soon, the **Thrive America Plan** bloomed into the **New York City Thrive America Plan**, a testament to a shared determination to forge a sustainable future. The city embraced our vision, and I felt the excitement of progress in every skyscraper, on every bustling street corner. Amidst it all, there was an indescribable feeling of collaboration and unity—a community finally taking charge of its own destiny.

Chapter 3 - The Interview

My daydreams shattered as the plane's wheels hit the tarmac with a soft thud. The sudden jolt was a gentle reminder that my journey into the past had come to an end, and the future was now a reality. The seatbelt light clicked on, and a chorus of passengers unbuckled, a collective sigh of relief and anticipation filling the cabin. I grabbed my carry-on bag, its weight a familiar comfort, and joined the flow of disembarking passengers.

The air in the terminal carried a quiet clarity, a stark contrast to the electric pulse of New York. There was a cool, measured efficiency here, echoing the serene Norwegian landscape beyond the glass. As I navigated toward baggage claim, anticipation and anxiety twined together inside me, old companions on the edge of something new. This city was a blank page, and though my past had shaped me, it offered no script for what lay ahead. At **Gate 4**, a sleek black sedan waited, just as the stewardess had promised, a silent invitation to the next chapter.

The chauffeur, a distinguished-looking man with a neatly trimmed beard, held a sign bearing my name. He smiled and said, "Dr. Caldwell? Welcome to Oslo." His voice was kind and reassuring, and his handshake was firm. As he led me through the bustling terminal, I could feel the eyes of other travelers on us, a silent curiosity about who I was and why I had a private car waiting for me. I felt a surge of pride, a quiet acknowledgment of how far I'd come from the girl who'd fled her home to find herself.

The car, a polished black Mercedes, glided through the city—a world away from the clattering taxis of New York. Inside, tranquility wrapped around me, broken only by the soft hum of the engine. The chauffeur let silence settle, giving me space to absorb the city's rhythm. We passed gleaming towers and lively plazas, living proof of the urban renewal I had once only dreamed of. Through the window, I glimpsed friends sharing laughter at a café and students deep in study on a sunlit bench. Their energy sparked memories of my own classroom, and the quiet pride of watching young minds awaken.

As we approached the center of the city, the chauffeur finally broke the silence. "The ceremony is tomorrow evening at the **Oslo Opera House**. It's a great honor what you've done for urban development." His words were sincere, and they resonated with a deep sense of purpose. I had poured my heart and soul into the **Thrive America Plan**, but it was only in this moment, in a foreign city, that I truly grasped its impact. This wasn't just about me or New York anymore. It was about an idea that had transcended borders, a vision of communities taking charge of their own destinies. The honor wasn't for me alone; it was for every person who had ever believed in the power of a single idea to change the world. The limousine pulled up to a grand hotel, and I took a deep breath. My journey was just beginning.

I had scarcely set my bag down in the Grand Hotel room when a sharp, purposeful knock echoed through the door. Opening it, I found a young Norwegian woman, her dark hair gleaming beneath the hallway's bright lights. A subtle trace of perfume lingered in the air as she offered a poised, courteous smile.

"Hi, Dr. Caldwell," she said, her voice soft but confident. "I am Birgit Makhom, your personal assistant for the next five days. There is a lot to cover. Most importantly, you have an interview with the British Broadcasting Company in thirty minutes." The realization hit me like a splash of cold water. My heart rate sped up, and for a moment, the room seemed to spin. Birgit's words cut through my surprise: "The interview room is off the lobby."

The hotel lobby thrummed with life—a symphony of hushed conversations, the gentle clink of glasses, and sudden bursts of laughter. Exhilaration and nerves tangled inside me, the very air humming with expectation. Inside the interview room, a tall, blond man—Jens—welcomed me with a genuine smile and a crisp Norwegian accent, motioning me to a seat as he sorted his notes. A woman swept over, dusting powder across my cheeks and adding a hint of lipstick. The lights blazed, and warmth pressed in from every side.

"Our conversation will begin shortly and will last about thirty minutes," Jens said. I couldn't help but wonder if he was aware of my history with the New York City Council.

After the introductions, the cameras started rolling. Jens leaned forward, his expression serious. "Dr. Caldwell, the City Council of New York targeted you with their opposition. Can you explain why?"

I shifted in my seat, taking a slow, steady breath. It was crucial to be direct and honest. "I should have seen it as a personal attack from the beginning," I said, a flicker of frustration in my voice. "The truth is, they weren't interested in supporting the success of my project. Their priority was passing legislation on their own terms, and they saw me and the **Thrive America Plan** as an obstacle."

Jens's eyes narrowed slightly. "Were you trying to exert control over the City Council? To force them to conform to your desires?"

"No," I said, shaking my head. "That was never my intent. But I did make it clear that the opinions of the people were more important than my own. We created an administrative arm for our organization, one that would diligently track its votes. We announced that the voting results would be published for everyone to see on our website." I paused, letting the statement hang in the air. "If they perceived that as a threat, that wasn't my intention. I was simply stating a fact. We're about transparency, not advocacy. We track the 'yes' or 'no' votes of every council member, and we occasionally publish that information. The program was never meant to be interpreted as a way to control them."

Jens nodded, processing my words. "Can you share with our audience how you got started with the **Thrive America Plan**, and what its core intentions are?"

"Well," I began, my tone softening as I moved to a more comfortable topic. "The entire journey started as a research project I did in the late 90s. The media was buzzing with discussions about term limits for Congress and the Supreme Court. While conducting my research, I rediscovered the ancient Greek democracy and its enduring influence on our modern political structure. It's entirely possible that our Founding Fathers delved into this very subject."

"So, it started as just an idea?" Jens prodded. "What steps did you take to turn it into something real?"

"For years, I struggled to figure out how to implement the concept," I admitted. "But I kept working on it in my mind as I taught. I began applying the ideas in my classroom, fostering a sense of collaboration. I created a template that ensured everyone had a voice in discussions. We would move around, refining our ideas in different groups. This approach yielded multidimensional results and made everyone feel included."

"And that classroom experience led to **TAP**?"

I nodded. "Yes. The core of **TAP** is the same idea. To explain how it works, let's look at the first round." I leaned forward, my hands gesturing as I spoke, the details of the program flowing from me with an effortless rhythm. "Community members sign up on a website, and when they arrive, we assign them a table based on their registration and address, giving them a card with a letter and a number. For the first round, they sit together in groups by number that correspond to their respective neighborhoods."

Jens held up a hand. "I don't understand how the numbering system works."

"It's quite simple," I said, smiling at his interjection. "Let's use the West Village as an example. The tables labeled by number correspond to the streets. All the people from 12th Street would sit at one table, 11th Street at another, and so on. They have 45 minutes to discuss the problems they want to see changed in their neighborhood, with the goal of identifying three key issues. Our facilitators make sure the session stays focused, preventing it from devolving into just storytelling or complaining. "

"After the 45 minutes are up, we give everyone electronic voting devices. They input their three issues, and we take a fifteen-minute break while the team compiles all the issues on a main board. We combine any repetitive issues into one." I paused, taking a sip of water. "I then present the consolidated list, and then comes the second round."

"The second round is a cross-section of the entire community. Everyone finds a new seat based on the letter on the back of their card, creating diverse groups that include representatives from every street. This cross-section then engages in a deeper discussion, trying to narrow down the list to three issues they believe are prevalent throughout the entire community, not just their specific neighborhood."

Jens's pen scribbled across his notepad. "And what happens after that? How do the issues get to City Hall?"

"That's a different process entirely," I said, a more thoughtful expression on my face. "My role is just to facilitate the facilitators and the groups. I am like a sturdy frame that envelops a vivid painting. The community is the vibrant painting itself—full of life and colors. They are the brushstrokes. I am simply the one who keeps it all intact. I introduce the community representatives to the City Council, but the people who represent the group are chosen by them."

Chapter 4 - The Conflict

Jens assumed responsibility for the interview, projecting a strong and determined demeanor. Demanding full attention, his voice cut through the air. He began his statement with an authoritative tone, informing everyone that Doctor Caldwell was going to reveal how the community selects their representatives. “Can you dive deeper into these groupings, untangling their intricate nuances?”

Jens’ commanding voice resonated through the vast room as he continued with the second question, bouncing off the ornate walls adorned with gilded tapestries. "Did the election of this community representative result in a conflict with City Hall?"

Taking a brief pause, I could sense the room's heavy anticipation, filled with hushed whispers and a lingering scent of nervousness. This issue had wrapped itself around City Hall's resistance like a thorny vine, almost choking the project's very existence. With the world's eyes upon me, I understood the importance of responding in a calculated, thoughtful, and carefully selected manner.

"In response to your question, Jens, about how we organized each community grouping, the process is actually quite simple. New York City divides into precincts, and they assign two police officers to each one. These officers serve as the link between the police department and the community. We believed it was crucial to involve the Police, Education, Fire, and Public Works Department. Our goal is to have these organizations actively participate by sending representatives to the community town hall meetings.

This approach has proven highly effective, as we now see genuine collaboration between the community and the governing bodies. Together, we are working towards creating secure and sustainable neighborhoods, presenting a united front.

Regarding your second question, I have to confess that it was a bit tricky. I was rather naïve and didn't anticipate such a response. I had assumed that

City Hall would embrace it with enthusiasm. However, certain members of the City Council felt threatened by this course of action."

Jens suddenly stopped me, his voice piercing the air. "But isn't this pushback justified?" he interrupted, his eyes narrowing in curiosity. "Isn't this representative essentially duplicating the responsibilities of city council members?"

Reflecting on the past, I responded by acknowledging the argument's validity. "However, it's crucial to highlight that ancient Greek democracy originally inspired the Thrive America Plan. In that system, all citizens actively took part in decision-making for their city-state, and there were term limits in place.

Upon conducting my research, I discovered these term limits existed to ensure that different members of the community had the opportunity to serve. It aimed to prevent the exclusive representation of the people's voice by career politicians who prioritize their self-interests. The ultimate goal was to avoid such a scenario completely.

Now, let me clarify I am not proposing that all City Council members seek election with the explicit goal of becoming career politicians. It is undeniable that certain members succumb to this temptation. Once they gain power, they come to recognize its importance and cling to it to validate their own self-worth. Regrettably, this undermines the entire democratic process."

After addressing these concerns, I proceeded to elucidate the process of electing representatives to the group. I suggested a representative should hold office for a specified duration of 18 months. The notion that continuity is crucial to support the role of a politician loses relevance in this specific context, since the entire community collectively determines the issues at hand.

The representative's primary responsibility is to advocate on behalf of the community and convey their concerns to the Council.

After the 18-month period elapses, the community selects a new representative to advocate for them. The sole prerequisite for this position is the capacity to address in three-minutes to the City Council during their bi-monthly meetings. To assist the representative with any work-related expenses, our organization, which operates as a nonprofit and relies on donations, provides a modest stipend. The representative will oversee the town hall gatherings and take on the responsibilities of being the facilitator, assuming my current role.

Once our group has established the dynamics within the community, the community itself will assume responsibility and manage their own affairs. The main objective of our program is to promote community involvement in day-to-day governance. However, we have encountered a challenge where some communities prefer to follow their own methods and not adhere to the template we have provided. There is no restriction preventing them from doing so. As mentioned earlier, our aim is for them to actively participate in their own governance. However, if they wish to receive our organization's support, including funding, it is crucial for them to utilize our template as a guide for their meetings.

I found it quite challenging to deal with this issue because, as both a facilitator and creator, I believed it was crucial to maintain a consistent structure throughout the entire city, benefiting all communities. Being knowledgeable in psychology, I was aware of how my ego could potentially influence my decision-making.

Before starting the program, I took a moment to pause and reflect. It dawned on me that, much like a picture frame, I needed to strike a harmonious balance between being adaptable and steadfast. Consequently, any community interested in participating in the Thrive America Plan had to make a written commitment to adhere to the established format. While acknowledging my own flaws, I also understood the significance of making future adjustments and fostering growth to create a more forward-thinking organization."

Lost in my thoughts, Jens abruptly cut me off, his eyes focused intently on the conversation. I could sense his growing enthusiasm in the way his brows furrowed and his voice filled the air.

I didn't wait for him to ask because we had already proven the success of TAP. I shared, "In fact, New York City alone has seen a reduction in crime of over 50% and an increase in community involvement by 95%. Our program's success has been so remarkable that communities in Boston, Philadelphia, Baltimore, Chicago, and Atlanta have sought our assistance. But what's even more impressive is our rapid expansion within New York City itself. In just a month, we were able to extend our reach from the West Village to Greenwich Village, Hell's Kitchen, Lolita, and Chelsea. Currently, almost 90% of the precincts have invested in our program."

After taking a few minutes to think, Jens finally mustered the courage to pose his question, his voice quivering slightly. “So, Doctor Caldwell, can you tell us about the initial pushback from City Council? And how did you navigate through it?”

Chapter 5 - The Pushback

Birgit entered the room with a graceful silence, her footsteps barely audible on the polished wood floor. She settled herself in the corner, a soft glow from the overhead light casting a gentle shadow over her poised figure. In her hands, her notebook lay open, ready to be filled with the final notes of our interview.

As my conversation with Jens drew to a close, the vibrant lights dimmed, wrapping the room in a cocoon of golden warmth. The soft creak of his chair echoed in the hush as he stood, nudging me to rise and seek out Birgit.

Her piercing gaze met mine, a subtle nod confirming the interview was over. A wave of relief washed over me, a feeling that Jens, too, seemed to share. He offered his genuine thanks, the quiet hum of the camera equipment filling the space behind his words.

A quiet sense of triumph shimmered in the air. I followed Jens, then floated toward Birgit, who welcomed me with a mischievous glint in her eyes.

"How was it, Doctor Caldwell?" she asked, her voice alive with curiosity.

"It was intense," I said, a sigh escaping my lips. I saw the exhaustion on her face, and a fresh wave of my own weariness hit me. "Birgit, can I just have some time alone? To unwind?"

She gave me a sympathetic look. "I'll take the lead on that. I've already had your clothes pressed and refreshed the itinerary. Tonight, there's a reception with the royal family and other dignitaries, followed by dinner. However, I've arranged a spa appointment for you—a massage, a mineral bath, and a complete hair and makeup treatment. You have an hour to yourself right now."

I thanked her, feeling relief surge through me. She slipped the schedule into my hand, the crisp white paper glowing softly in the dim hallway. With a gentle insistence, she entered her number into my phone, a silent vow of support. "Call me whenever you need anything," she said.

Back in my room, I closed the door, sealing out the last, spectral wisps of Norwegian winter. I shed my clothes, wrapped myself in a robe, and let my body melt into the bed. Exhaustion draped over me, thick and unyielding, coaxing me toward sleep, but my mind spun restlessly. Memories of the project's near-collapse swirled around me, sharp and fresh as open wounds.

I can never forget my first time presenting TAP to the Community. The event was held in Hell's Kitchen, and the room was buzzing with a sense of hope. News had spread that the community was ready to embrace the **Thrive America Plan**. But as people filed in, registering and finding their seats, I noticed a small group lingering at the back, their expressions cold and detached. I approached them, and to my surprise, I found they were city officials.

The room quieted as I began my presentation. But I was cut off, right in the middle, by a woman who stormed from the back of the room. I later learned she was Councilwoman Jelana White, the district's representative.

"Excuse me," I said, interrupting her. "May I ask what your intentions are?"

She seemed taken aback. "I am Councilwoman White. This is my district."

"I am aware of that," I said, "but this is a community event for members of this community. I'd ask you to please take a seat at the back and observe. This is not a platform for grandstanding."

Enraged, she marched toward me and stomped her foot, a sound that cracked in the sudden silence of the room. She insisted she had the authority to speak. But I stood my ground, my voice calm. "Do you also reside in this district?" I asked.

"Absolutely," she snapped back.

"Then I suggest you go to the registration table and get your card," I said. "Once you have it, you'll be assigned a table where you can wait for your turn to speak with your neighbors. Your voice is important, but it is just one of many."

My suggestion threw her off balance. Disbelief flickered across her face as she realized I would not bow to her demands. Tension crackled as our argument escalated, neither of us willing to yield. Her eyes blazed, but beneath the fire, I glimpsed uncertainty. At last, she retreated to the back, her entourage in tow. Relief surged through me. I had faced down a notorious bully, and the community had seen it.

That night, the community's frustration and fierce hope for change resonated deep within me. I left the meeting buoyed by their support, a new fire kindling in my chest. Armed with facts, data, and the will of the people, I steeled myself for the next battle: facing the City Council.

Tuesday came, and I went to City Hall. It was the third time I had been there, and I was scheduled to present my three-minute dissertation. I stood at the podium, ready to speak. The light box had a red and green light, and an LED screen showed a countdown. But the light never turned green.

"You've already presented this information," the clerk said, his voice cold. "We won't be giving you another chance to speak. There are others waiting."

I was in disbelief. "Are you telling me I can't speak at a City Council meeting? It's my right as a resident of this city."

The clerk stood tall, his voice cutting through the hushed room. "Dr. Caldwell, I'm sorry, but no. We will not be turning your microphone on. The code grants us the right." The representative who stood behind me, a proud community member, had his microphone shut off as well, the clicking sound a small, vicious defeat.

"You can't do that," I said, a low growl in my voice. "The program's purpose is to give people a voice!"

The Chair of the Council, a stoic woman with a sour expression, cut me off. "That's how things are done here."

That was the last straw. Even with my microphone muted, my voice, honed from years as a cheerleader, carried. "You all remain secluded in your ivory towers, crafting legislation that benefits yourselves, not the people!" I yelled, my voice echoing. "It is time for the consistent and unconditional expression of the people's voices to be heard!"

But I faced rejection from the Council. I later learned that Councilwoman White was the one behind it, determined to shut down TAP permanently. The news, of course, made headlines, but it was all negative.

White's office had fed biased talking points to the media, creating a skewed narrative. For days, the stories painted me as a disruptive, entitled activist.

No one called. No one wanted to hear my side. Silence pressed in, dense and suffocating, leaving me stranded with the weight of it all. Even now, sprawled in this hotel room, the ache of betrayal lingers, whispering through the quiet.

But then came the surprise. A prominent lawyer and his wife, both of whom had been at our West Village meeting in disguise, reached out to me. They commended my refusal to play the victim and assured me of their influential connections. Brian Saltsman, the lawyer, understood the wisdom of our program. We were promoting unity, not division.

After a month of tense negotiations, Brian finally broke through. I gathered the community to share the long-awaited good news. I apologized for the hardships and thanked them for their unwavering loyalty. Deep within, I unearthed a truth: a dream worth chasing is a living force, luminous and worthy of every struggle.

I was no longer fighting alone. Though some had drifted away, the heart of our program pulsed on, strong and unyielding. At the next meeting, their support rose around me like a tide. The room vibrated with new resolve, a symphony of unity. And thrive it did.

Knowing that Councilwoman White wouldn't go quietly by simply shutting the door, I knew fully that I was facing a multitude of antagonistic forces. With this in mind, I mentally braced myself for the challenge ahead. Equipped with solid facts, data, and the understanding that the public was in favor of this outcome, I fortified myself for the battle ahead.

However, just like many of her predecessors, once she took office, her priorities shifted towards using bullying tactics to ensure the passage of her legislation. She rarely interacted with the community, except for the period just before elections, when she would put on a performance, making promises that catered to their desires. Unfortunately, she often disregarded these promises after being elected. It perplexes me that people cannot see through this façade and not vote for politicians who consistently cannot fulfill their commitments. I also sympathize with those who struggle to make ends meet, as they find it challenging to summon the energy to take action at the end of each exhausting day. This is where someone like TAP comes into play, bringing about change and instilling hope in their lives.

After resolving the issues, it was time to choose a representative for our first town hall meeting. I carefully reviewed the instructions and exchanged phone numbers with the chosen representative to ensure we were well-prepared for the upcoming City Hall meeting on Tuesday. With the councilwoman gone, we wasted no time in transforming the back of the room into a private area for our discussion. Many people approached me to offer congratulations for standing up. The councilwoman had gained a reputation for being a tough bully, and they had elected her hoping she would continue to advocate forcefully on their behalf.

However, when Tuesday came I was taken me by surprise. It was the third instance where I found myself at the microphone, presenting my three-minute dissertation. It might have appeared monotonous, but I held the belief that repetition would make it resonate, considering my three minutes seemed to be directed at empty space. Finally, they announced the public comments. With eagerness, I stood up to secure my place at the front of the line. The representative was right behind me.

So, when I reached the microphone at the podium, I noticed a light-box displaying red and green lights, along with an LED screen showing the countdown. As I stood there, the light remained red, and

I patiently waited for it to turn green so I could begin speaking. However, to my surprise, the light never changed. They informed me I had already presented the information and they wouldn't give me another chance to speak. There were others waiting in line. I was in disbelief and asked, "Are you telling me I'm not allowed to speak at a city council meeting? I am a resident of this city. Is it not my entitlement to have the freedom of speech?"

The clerk stood upright, his voice cutting through the hushed atmosphere of the room. "Doctor Caldwell," he said, his tone filled with regret, "I'm sorry, but no, we will not be turning your microphone on. Code grants us the right. Yet, someone promptly silenced the representative's who stood after me, His microphone, also was shut off and the click resonated in the room.

The program's purpose was to provide the public with a voice in the City Council's decision-making I internalized. However, my previous confrontation carried significant consequences. "You can't possibly do that," I responded, challenging the assertion I was being disruptive.

In a disapproving tone, the Chair stated that's how things are done. I responded angrily, "You all remain secluded in your ivory towers, crafting legislation that primarily benefits yourselves, rather than the people. It is high time for the City Council to prioritize the desires and necessities of the citizens. It is now time for the consistent and unconditional expression of the people's voices to be heard." Even though the microphone had been muted, as a cheerleader in my youth, I knew how to project my voice.

Councilwoman White, her presence commanding, dared to break the silence. She had attended our meeting with a singular purpose - to listen to the concerns and issues of her district. No one needed to present anything to her; she was there, ready to absorb every word.

I faced rejection from the Council, and I learned that Councilman White was the one behind permanently shutting me down, determined to do the same for the

TAP program. As expected, this news made headlines, but the coverage was mostly negative. The media received biased talking points from Councilman White's office, which resulted in skewed reporting in her favor.

Negative reports filled the media for days, even extending into the weekend. Before long, I started getting phone calls from community members and our representative, who all believed that our efforts were a total waste of time. The City Council had no interest in letting us represent the community or bring our concerns to their attention. The presence of TAP only reinforced this as a vote of lack of confidence, leaving many feeling offended.

No one reached out to interview or inquire about my perspective. The silence echoed in my mind, leaving me alone, deep in contemplation. The weight of the situation enveloped me. Reliving all of this, I lay in my dimly lit hotel room, casting long shadows on the walls, while the faint scent of hotel linens lingered in the air. Thoughts swirled in my head like a whirlwind of emotions and unanswered questions. Amid it all, I couldn't help but marvel at the incredible power of life, which had somehow orchestrated this extraordinary turn of events.

In the West Village community, there was a prominent lawyer and his wife who were present in disguise. Despite their affluence, they reached out to me after following the news and claimed to understand the underlying truth of what had occurred. They commended my refusal to play the victim's card and assured me of their influential connections. With their assistance, they pledged to exert pressure on the City Council to acknowledge our organization and its objectives.

Acknowledging the importance of collaboration between both parties, Brian Saltsman, a lawyer, recognized the significance and wisdom of our program. We promoted unity rather than perpetuate division. Although it took an additional month of negotiations, He eventually achieved progress. To keep everyone informed about the advancements, I arranged another community meeting. My aim was to inspire and maintain the ongoing support from our representative. I expressed remorse for any difficulties encountered and expressed gratitude for their steadfast commitment to the cause.

In the depths of my soul, I felt a profound understanding that a dream worth pursuing was akin to a Majestic Being worth battling for. I wasn't fighting this battle alone during this moment of my existence. Despite the loss of a fraction of our community, the program remained intact, unyielding. At the reinforced meeting, I could sense the palpable support and unwavering defense from those around me, their steadfast belief in the cause. The atmosphere crackled with determination, resonating with the symphony of voices, creating a harmonious symphony of solidarity. And, oh, how it thrived, filling the air with a vibrant energy that permeated every sens

Chapter 6 The First Amendment

The soft glow of the dimmed lights enveloped the massage room, casting gentle shadows on the walls. The warmth of the oil seeped into my skin, its soothing aroma filling the air. As the firm, gentle pressure of skilled hands worked on my back, I felt the knots of fear and doubt, the ones that had plagued me since the interview, slowly begin to unravel. Each rhythmic stroke was a symphony of sound, a melody of release. This weekend had pushed me to my limits, but in this tranquil moment, I found solace.

My mind, however, would not rest. It wandered from the interview to the long nights spent hunched over my dissertation on societal change. I had braced myself for resistance, but I was unprepared for the shadowy maneuvers and ruthless politics that followed. The Chair of the Council, radiating authority, demanded unwavering loyalty to block the Thrive America Plan, warning that anyone who defied her would risk their position. The air in the room grew thick with fear.

A voice, someone on the inside, later told me exactly what had been said: “Standing at the podium, she declared the creation of a data-gathering branch. The threat lingered as she warned of using this information against us if we resisted." Brian Saltsman had tried to reassure me that this information would serve as our defense, but the Council's actions brought the wrath of every influence they had down upon me. Since our organization depended on donations, I watched in horror as our bottom line plunged into the negative.

The therapist's hands pressed into a stubborn knot beneath my shoulder blade, making me flinch. The ache in my body mirrored the sting of old wounds. I felt hollowed out, my mind and spirit drained. Depression crept in, heavy and relentless. I had crashed to my lowest point. Waves of self-doubt, always lurking beneath the surface, now threatened to drown me. My training in psychology reminded me that naming the darkness was the first step to dispelling it. Yet the barrage of slanted news stories, the relentless negative press—carefully orchestrated by the City Council—was taking its toll.

The deepest wound was not the public slander or the financial losses. It was watching community members distance themselves, branding us a "failing organization." Their words echoed the disappointment of our donors. TAP existed to lift the community, and seeing them abandon hope for change shattered me. The pain twisted inside me, sharp and unrelenting.

I struggled to keep the organization afloat, pinching every penny, but I was fraying at the edges. I nearly gave up. Logic urged me to protect myself, to walk away. Yet this project was woven into my very being. It felt inseparable from who I was. Still, a haunting sense of déjà vu crept in, whispering that this venture might end like the last—a bold, solitary gamble.

Back then, I had poured every cent I owned into challenging the final fortress of the billionaire boys club, only to be shut out before I could even make my case. They cut me off without warning, leaving me in financial freefall.

That plunge into the abyss taught me a hard lesson: I would never again risk everything to the point of bankruptcy. With that resolve, I started making plans to shut down my venture for good.

Just as I was about to quit, a call arrived. It was the Law Offices of Brian Saltsman. I walked into their midtown office, nervous, only to be surprised by the partners who were waiting for me. They were all members of the West Village community, people we had brought online through our project. They believed in our vision. In an instant, a wave of relief washed over me, lifting the heavy burden I had carried for months.

"The Council infringed upon your First Amendment rights," Brian said. They had obtained video evidence of all my presentations to the Council, which showed no sign of anger, rudeness, or disruptive conduct. They had a complaint drafted and were eager to present it to the City Council. The lawyers instructed me to go back to City Hall and present any new representatives.

I was delighted to secure commitments from Lenox Hill, Yorkville, and even a portion of Carnegie Hill, an area of the Upper East Side I had expected to resist change. It was here that I found my guardian angel: Mike Stein, a well-liked former mayor and a close friend of Brian. The residents elected Mike as the representative for the Carnegie Hill area, and I decided he would be the first one introduced at the next meeting.

As I left the law firm, a seasoned partner in her seventies named Marjorie Lord beckoned me into the dimly lit hallway. With an unwavering gaze, she clenched her fist and struck her palm, the sound echoing in the corridor. Her piercing eyes locked onto mine.

"You, my friend, are a true New Yorker," she said in a resolute voice. "That means you confront adversity head-on, with unwavering tenacity. You embrace every challenge and you conquer it fearlessly. Now, go out there and exhibit the mettle that defines you."

Her words struck a chord, jolting me from my gloom. I chose to walk home, savoring the perfect New York evening, the air crisp and invigorating. As I left Midtown for Yorkville, each step seemed to unlock a new piece of the city. Marjorie Lord's words lingered, echoing in my heart.

I thought of Jimi Hendrix's words: "There won't be peace in the world until the power of love overcomes the love of power." It hit me like a lightning bolt. I had been fighting for the people's voice to be heard, for them to realize their worth and value. I had been their advocate. Now, it was time for me to practice what I preached and have faith in my own abilities.

Chapter 7 Corruption

The call came, and I answered. It was Brian Saltsman, and his voice was low, conspiratorial. "Mike wants to meet. He says it needs to be confidential. He's inviting us to his home for dinner." He would pick me up at precisely six o'clock.

As I waited, Marjorie's words echoed in my mind. "New York tough." I had to know what it meant. Was it a bully's aggressive pushback, a win-at-all-costs mentality? Or was it something else entirely—a quiet, unwavering resolve in the face of impossible odds?

We arrived at Mike's luxurious townhome on Fifth Avenue and 88th Street. The staff led us to the drawing room, a sprawling space where drinks and hors d'oeuvres were spread out like a royal feast. We were only a few sips into our Manhattans when Mike entered. He was all charm, gesturing to a pair of leather armchairs. "Plenty to share," he said, his smile not quite reaching his eyes.

He started with a question that felt like a test. "What do you know about Hell's Kitchen?"

"It's near the theater district," I replied. "The area between 34th and 59th streets."

"Yes," he said, leaning back. "But what else? It's a place where city zoning typically limits buildings to six stories.[1] Many are undesirable walk-up apartments. Historically, it was the grimiest, filthiest part of the city. A New York Times reporter in 1881 interviewed a rookie cop who described a multiple murder scene there as a 'blistering inferno.' The reporter scoffed, 'This is no ordinary Hell. It's like stepping into Hell's kitchen.' That name stuck."

He took a slow drink of his Manhattan, his eyes fixed on me. "It was a stronghold for underprivileged Irish Americans, but with a notable presence of Latino Americans. And that's where your girl hails from—Councilwoman Jelana White. She's a tenacious New Yorker who tirelessly engaged with the Latino community, making big promises to get a seat on the council. They trusted her, and she won."

Mike leaned forward, his voice dropping to a near-whisper. "Because of its gritty reputation, the real estate prices stayed low. It attracted artists, but a slow shift in demographics has begun. Recently, the City Council—50 members strong—passed a new redistricting map. They have the power to do this, and it's where corruption thrives. In the early 1980s, they granted each council member the authority to redraw their own district. It's a system designed to give them almost uncontested power and zero accountability."

The truth landed like a blow to the ribs. My grip tightened around my glass, knuckles whitening. Brian drained his drink, his gaze locked on Mike, searching for answers.

"A council member takes a bribe to approve a zoning change or turn a blind eye to a building inspection," Mike continued, his voice as flat and cold as a sheet of ice. "They line their pockets, but to enjoy it, they have to stay in office. They manipulate the district boundaries—they literally chose their own voters."

My voice cut through the air, clear and sharp. "You're saying they're selecting their own constituents, not the other way around. And they use these carefully crafted maps for political gain. It's a power grab."

"Exactly," Mike said. "They view any requirements as obstacles. Their main concern is reelection, so they lock a district in for a decade with no regard for the residents' needs. That's why your **TAP** program is so important. It's the reason I'm here. Because as you immerse yourself in the chaos, you'll begin to understand why both you and your organization pose a formidable threat to the illicit power they've usurped."

Brian added, his tone more personal, "Have you ever noticed how most politicians look down on people? They wear tailored suits, but they're still condescending. There's a scent of superiority that just… lingers."

Brian's words struck a chord deep within me, stirring memories of my father's gaze when I was a girl—his queenie, destined to command, even when the world doubted.

"An interesting perception," Mike replied. "I suppose I was considered one of 'them.' But let me share what I've discovered from my sources. Several members gathered secretly to discuss the map situation. They made a pact to support each other and ensure their constituents' loyalty, guaranteeing their reelection."

He paused, letting the silence build. "Someone secretly recorded the entire meeting. I have read the transcripts, and they are damning. They're filled with slurs against ethnic groups. The recording is in a secure location, and no one can know about it until we release it."

Mike's gaze sharpened. "The head of the Local 831 union—the sanitation workers—attended the meeting. This union has over 12,000 members and immense influence. The city is facing a major rat problem and inconsistent garbage pickup, and this is a hot issue for your organization to tackle."

He pulled out a tablet and swiped to a video. "This was sent to me by a community member." The video was a grainy, 63-second clip. It showed a Sanitation

Department truck in Brooklyn, its workers collecting most of the refuse, but as they drove away, numerous bags tumbled out. The workers briefly stopped, glanced back, and then drove off, leaving behind a trail of trash, milk cartons, and cardboard boxes. The perfect breeding ground for rats.

I felt a surge of cold fury. "They're involved," I stated. "They're turning a blind eye to this."

Mike put the tablet away, his expression grim. "They've infiltrated the council. They have a deal. It's not just incompetence, Max. It's a conspiracy. And you're about to expose it. You have to address this issue with the City Council. The politicians who hold the majority vote will not support you."

The savory aroma of dinner hung in the air, but any hunger I felt had vanished. Mike's words had stripped away the last illusions. My battle was not with a handful of crooked officials, but with a machine built to protect itself. This was a fight against a power structure that prized self-preservation over the city's soul. This, I realized, was the heart of being "New York tough": not just resisting, but rising to confront a relentless tide of corruption.

Chapter 8 The Beast's Belly

As we gathered around the dinner table, the soft glow of the chandelier illuminated the room, creating a warm and inviting atmosphere. The clinking of silverware against plates mingled with the low hum of conversation, but all eyes were on Mike. He was a natural storyteller, and his voice, though gentle, carried a weight of authority.

He started with an example that seemed innocuous. "Let's talk about getting a liquor license for a restaurant," he began. "There's a strict cap on them. This creates a black market for so-called 'unauthorized' licenses that can cost upwards of $350,000. So, as a restaurant owner, it's not enough to have capital. You have to have **connections**."

I leaned forward, intrigued. "So, you're saying it's not just a matter of paying off an official, but navigating a system that's designed to be difficult?"

"Exactly," Mike said, a knowing look in his eyes. He recounted a specific case where a local police department had been expediting gun license approvals in exchange for political favors. "The FBI got involved," he said, and for a moment, the air grew thick with a sense of unspoken warning. The room fell silent as he described the elaborate schemes he had uncovered, a palpable scent of deception and greed in his words.

He revealed how builders, developers, and business owners found themselves trapped, forced to grease palms for zoning changes, building permits, and every city hurdle in their path. Sometimes the demands were blunt, other times they hung in the air, a silent but unmistakable price for progress.

"Now, let's shift back to Hell's Kitchen," Mike continued, a sharp edge in his voice. "It's an area primed for revitalization, and your Councilwoman, Jelana White, knows it. She wants to leave her mark, and she sees you as a roadblock. But she might not know that there are plans in motion to replace her with a white male from the thriving LGBTQ community. From what I gather, her time is running out, and her desperation makes her dangerous."

I watched as the puzzle pieces snapped into place: the ruthless power plays, the sly redrawing of district lines, the quiet terror of politicians clinging to their seats. Every move seemed to feed the same insatiable beast of corruption.

"You'll encounter this corruption everywhere, not just with residents," Mike said, his voice dropping to a low rumble. "You'll have to interact with business owners who have already fulfilled their 'obligations.' They will resist any change that might disrupt the status quo. Change is the key factor here."

He laid out the corruption in stark, chilling detail: "One element is the exchange of favors for a sweetheart contract, a specific law, or a required permit. It's all in exchange for cash and gifts. In another district, karaoke bar owners were extorted for their liquor licenses, and a council member demanded personal favors from them, threatening raids if they refused."

He then described the "pay-to-play" scandals. "Picture a dimly lit council chamber," he said, his voice taking on the cadence of a narrator. "A council member, with a sly grin, shamelessly extorts cash or campaign contributions. Licenses, permits, and other approvals are pawns in this game of greed."

Mike connected this to the bigger picture, mentioning a massive low-income housing tax credit scandal in another city where 14 individuals, including a state representative, were found guilty of extortion. "From my perspective," he said, looking at me directly, "corruption within local governments is widespread throughout the United States. In New York City, the problem lies in the permitting and licensing processes for startups and the restaurant industry."

He rattled off the daunting list: up to 30 permits, 23 separate inspections, each one another hurdle for a hopeful restaurateur. "The process drags on for an average of 225 days. It's a gauntlet meant to exhaust newcomers and reward only the seasoned survivors. The system is built to break your spirit before you even begin."

Mike recounted the story of a couple from San Francisco who signed a lease and invested their life savings after being told they qualified for an expedited process. "Six months later, they were told the city had 'misunderstood' the new law, and their permits were revoked. Corruption casts a shadow of uncertainty over every business owner. They sign leases and allocate money, but when the launch is postponed, their financial burden intensifies. They're spending money without generating any revenue, sinking into a deficit before their doors even open."

He finished with a final, chilling example of a Los Angeles restaurateur who ran for City Council after waiting 2.5 years for permits. "Independent chefs and restaurant owners find it nearly impossible to get liquor licenses," Mike explained. "This is a major source of frustration for officials, and you'll find yourself facing opposition in the City Council. Each member is focused on protecting their own interests and supporting one another, leaving you feeling cornered."

Mike's words revealed a system not accidentally flawed, but meticulously engineered for corruption. Every official's whim, every arbitrary license cap, every sluggish step in the bureaucracy was a brick in a fortress built to shelter the powerful.

He met my gaze, his eyes filled with a new kind of urgency. "Speaking of which, we can't let them win.

Now you understand what you're up against, Maxine. You must expose all of this. The public needs to know."

"Shall we move on to dessert?" Mike asked, but his words hinted at more than just the next course. As a gentle sweetness drifted through the air and we moved toward the parlor, I realized the real challenge was just beginning, and it would be anything but sugar-coated.

Chapter 9 The Rise Above

The deep crimson port in my glass shimmered with the promise of indulgence. I let its velvet richness linger on my tongue, then followed with a chocolate truffle that melted away all tension. For a fleeting moment, bliss wrapped around me—until the spotlight shifted, and it was my turn to speak.

"Mike," I began, my voice soft but firm. "I'm genuinely grateful for this conversation. I can be a bit naive at times, and you've truly opened my eyes to new perspectives. But I need to clarify something for both of you. In my younger years, I would have been fiercely determined to expose this corruption myself. And I still believe it needs to be brought to light. But it's not my responsibility to be the one to do it."

I leaned forward, my hands flat on the table, willing them to understand my conviction. "I've worked hard to conquer my personal inclination to lash out and fight for justice. Now, I'm channeling that energy in a different way. I'm not the hero; I'm the catalyst. The people will be the driving force behind this change."

I took a deep breath. "TAP will gather data on how every council member votes. I won't tell people how to vote—that's their decision. However, the information will be available, providing a roadmap for them to either bring about change or maintain the status quo. Sticking with the status quo will not get them the change they demand. I am merely an observer, a facilitator in this magnificent orchestration of events."

"Brian," I said, turning to him. "What is your opinion on whether the Council, under Councilwoman White's leadership, infringed upon my First Amendment rights?"

Brian's expression was serious. "We have all the tapes and recordings. There's no evidence to support their claims that you were unruly. So, yes, they did. Are you ready to proceed?"

"Max, don't you feel any responsibility to expose Jelana White?" Mike interjected, a hint of frustration in his voice.

"Unfortunately, I don't."

"I think you should reconsider," he pushed, his voice loud and commanding, interrupting the peaceful silence.

"I have," I answered firmly, my voice resolute. The weight of responsibility settled on my shoulders, a reminder of my mission to ensure this organization's success. "If someone violated my First Amendment rights, I will fight with every fiber of my being. And I implore you both to join me. But I'm hesitant to go beyond that box. If I pursue this corruption angle, the council's objections will attract federal attention. The FBI will intervene, and indictments will follow. If the public truly wants progress, they must vote people like her out. The responsibility lies on their shoulders."

"Gentlemen, are you still willing to support me?"

"Definitely," Brian exclaimed. "I'm excited to see TAP implemented in my neighborhood and across the city."

"Mike?"

He looked at me, a flicker of disappointment in his eyes. "Though I'm disappointed, my support for TAP remains unwavering. The journey may be longer, but I see the authenticity behind this endeavor. I am with you."

"By me standing on a pedestal and pushing for accountability, I put the project at risk," I explained.

"For substantial, lasting change, we need widespread community support; otherwise, everything is in jeopardy. This change is something I want to see in all cities."

"From where I stand," Mike said, his tone softening, "I offer my full support. I'm compelled to stand by your side."

"Great," Brian said, standing up. "It's time to go."

"Thank you, Mike," I said, rising to my feet. "The dinner was lovely, and our conversation was informative. This helps me understand how to move forward. Believe, Mike. Believe in this process. I know this is the key." I said goodnight.

The ride home unfolded to the city's nightly symphony—the low hum of traffic, the wail of distant sirens weaving through the darkness. Brian's silence was companionable, a quiet that settled warmly between us. As we reached my door, he turned with a reassuring smile. "Hey Max, goodnight! Just wanted to remind you to stay strong. Don't give up, keep pushing forward. I'll call you next week. Night."

Gratitude surged within me, buoyed by the steadfast support I had received. Confidence, once flickering, now glowed brighter as I crossed my threshold. I paused, recognizing the transformation within myself. Another challenge loomed ahead, but this time, I felt ready to weather any storm. As I sank into my pillow, a profound sense of purpose settled over me. The urge to be a hero still stirred inside—not for applause, but for my own evolution. I finally understood that real heroism is found in mastering the restless need for validation.

Chapter 10 Comeuppance

I arrived early for the City Council meeting on Tuesday, my first in two months. Uncertainty gnawed at me—would I even be allowed to speak? The public had been warned of a closed session to start things off, so patience became my silent companion. We all sat, waiting, anticipation thick in the air.

I felt certain the council was poring over the documents my lawyers had delivered, exposing their violation of my First Amendment rights. The lawsuit demanded compensation for the two months during which I had been silenced, a period when every donation had vanished. The sum was modest, but to me, it stood for justice.

I had discovered the council's latest tactic: planting agitators in our meetings to stir up chaos with unruly outbursts. Yet Marjorie's advice rang in my ears—resilience is the mark of a true New Yorker. I drew on my days teaching in Atlantic City's toughest neighborhoods, where every voice mattered, even the loudest dissenters. By standing close, I offered a silent challenge that unsettled them. Their attempts at disruption faded as they realized their words, too, were being heard.

As I braced for the hostility I knew was coming, Brian quietly took the seat beside me. Moments later, Mike settled in on my other side. We formed a united front in the first row. When the Council finally emerged, their eyes landed on us at once. A ripple of surprise swept across their faces as they caught sight of Mike.

Once the Council took its seats, we all rose together to recite the Pledge of Allegiance. As the agenda unfolded, I could feel their eyes flicker toward me; their voices were tinged with a wariness that had replaced the open animosity. For the first time, it seemed they feared me more than I feared them.

The room brimmed with people, rows upon rows stretching behind me like a living tide. I could not count them all, but their presence was undeniable. The air crackled with energy, and as I breathed it in, tears pricked my eyes. I was not alone. I belonged to a community united by a common cause.

When my moment arrived, I gathered every shred of courage and stepped forward. The microphone glowed green, signaling that my voice mattered. With pride, I announced Mike Stein as our first representative for Carnegie Hill. The Council's rules demanded silence—no applause, no cheers, no shouts of support. Still, in that hush, we discovered a quiet, powerful unity.

As I turned to return to my seat, a breathtaking sight unfolded before me. The crowd, steadfast and resolute, rose as one. Not a word was uttered, not a single cheer broke the silence. It was a stunning, wordless declaration—a sea of people standing shoulder to shoulder in perfect accord. The room pulsed with unity and determination, the very air charged with their shared conviction. The silent strength of our solidarity was a reckoning the Council never anticipated.

Chapter 11 -New York Tough

The soft glow of the ambient music played in my room as Birgit and I settled down to review my speech. The tranquility of the spa had calmed my mind, but the weight of my upcoming address still lingered. My speech was not just about the **Thrive America Plan**; it was about its core principle of peacekeeping. I wanted to clarify that this organization, born out of conflict, was established to promote collaboration and unity, rather than escalate disputes. It was the epitome of what Marjorie had called **New York Tough**—not being a bully, but standing firm in your convictions without compromising your integrity.

Birgit's phone rang, and she held it to her ear, her brow furrowed. "It's Jens Christensen," she whispered, her eyes wide. She hung up, a look of intrigue on her face. "He wants to know if you have an escort for tonight's ceremony."

I was stunned. Our interviews had been so formal, so professional. I replayed our conversations in my mind, searching for a sign of his interest. Why would he want to escort me? Was he simply being kind, or was he digging for a scoop? Was I just a part of a story he wanted to tell?

A sense of loneliness washed over me. I had achieved so much, but I had done it alone. I had no one by my side to share this incredible journey with. "It's obvious that I'm the only person here without an escort," I admitted, a hint of vulnerability in my voice. "And frankly, I'm tired of being alone."

I looked at Birgit, a smile slowly spreading across my face. "Please, tell Jens I'd love for him to be my escort. We'll meet in the hotel lobby at the time you decide. I assume a luxurious limousine awaits us?"

A small smile played on Birgit's lips. "I'm not sure if he'd prefer to meet here or at the event itself. But I'll call him to clarify. I can already tell he'll be ecstatic to hear your answer."

Chapter 12 - The Key to Peace

My palms were damp with sweat as I sat there, my stomach a tangled knot of nerves. Jens noticed the tension, but he remained silent, offering a calming presence. I fidgeted, my fingers tapping on the table, barely grazing the untouched plate of food. I took a sip of water, and then I saw Birgit making her way toward me, her heels clicking on the polished floor.

"It's time," she whispered, her voice filled with concern. "They want you queued up to speak. You hardly ate? Are you okay?"

"Yes," I said, my voice shaky. "Just a jumble of nerves."

I ascended the backstage stairs, each step swallowed by the plush carpet as I rehearsed my speech in my mind. Drawing in a steadying breath, I heard my name announced, the words drifting past like a far-off melody. The stage lights blazed before me, casting dramatic shadows on the velvet curtains. Heart pounding, I stepped into the glow, greeted by a wave of applause. My voice found its place.

"What does it mean to thrive? How does it differ from surviving?" I asked, my voice gaining strength with each word. "Surviving is a weak heartbeat, simply persisting. But thriving, ah, that's a symphony. It's the sight of vibrant colors painting our cityscape, the sound of laughter, and the aroma of freshly scented flora mingling with the morning air. It's an energy that surges through your veins, propelling you forward."

I paused, letting the silence hang in the air. "So, I have to ask: was New York City truly thriving before the creation of **TAP**? Or were its inhabitants just surviving, their lives overshadowed by fear and reliance on the routine?" I let my gaze sweep across the audience. "The very idea of a life beyond mere survival brings us closer to the allure of thriving. Who wouldn't want that?"

I described how a vibrant community dances with change, spotting opportunities and shifting strategies to seize the best outcomes. "But adaptability isn't easy," I admitted. "We cling to the familiar, holding tight to the status quo because it feels safe. Yet that comfort can become a cage, keeping us from truly thriving."

I delved into the underlying issues, the ones that create obstacles to progress. "Movements like **TAP** are disruptive by nature," I explained. "They challenge the old ways of managing urban environments. They inspire profound transformations and promote a sense of togetherness and solidarity. One of the major obstacles is government red tape, and the dysfunctionality of the City Council often exacerbates that burden. Why? Because council members prioritize their position and status over the needs of their constituents."

I continued, my voice unwavering. "A small council of legislators can create a powerful pressure to conform. Many individuals conform to the group, even if it means disregarding their own thoughts and potential consequences. This is **Groupthink.**" I let the term hang in the air, a familiar concept without a formal explanation. "They perceive differing viewpoints as acts of disloyalty. This collective decision-making, based on fear and conformity, can have disastrous results."

"**TAP** seeks to bridge that gap," I said, a sense of purpose filling me. "It establishes a collaborative framework. It's a platform for the community to voice their opinions on how they want change. By embracing the concept of **TAP**, a city becomes more receptive to fresh ideas, fostering creativity and innovation. Even in chaotic circumstances, this approach allows for problem-solving. It means asking, 'What's the opportunity?'"

I ended with a powerful message. "Resilient and flourishing individuals can become inspiring leaders, guiding others through the most challenging circumstances. When the entire community prospers, the City flourishes. Instead of fixating on daily hardships, the community asks, 'What strengths do I possess that I can contribute?' And when everyone lends a hand, managing becomes less burdensome."

The sound of Jimi Hendrix's guitar still echoed in my mind, a perfect harmony for my words: *"There will be peace when the power of love overcomes the love of power."*

I drifted off the stage, buoyed by the roar of applause that seemed to lift me above the crowd. Sinking into my seat, hunger crashed over me, and I eagerly devoured the meal Jens had guarded for me. "You can call me Max," I said, shedding the weight of formality in the glow of celebration.

Just as the idea settled in, Jens's gentle touch on my arm startled me. Amidst the chaos and noise in the Hall, his words, barely audible, pierced through.

"The BBC offered me a position in New York City."

A jolt of excitement and anticipation raced through me, impossible to contain. I had been handed a key to the city, and perhaps, just perhaps, a new beginning, possibly a key to my heart.

www.ingramcontent.com/pod-product-compliance
Lightning Source LLC
Chambersburg PA
CBHW010356310726
48979CB00006B/1059

* 9 7 8 0 9 8 3 5 6 4 7 8 2 *